THIS BOOK
BELONGS TO

_____

_____

A LITTLE OWL BOOK

HEIDI

retold by Hilda Young
illustrated by Susan Aspey

WORLD

One bright morning a little girl walked hand in hand with her aunt up a steep path in the Swiss mountains.

Aunt Dete was taking Heidi to the home of her grandfather who lived all alone in a hut at the top of the Alm.

Heidi's grandfather was very surprised to see them, and at first he did not want Heidi to stay. But when Heidi smiled at him and put her hands in his, the Alm Uncle relented, and let Heidi stay.

He made Heidi a soft bed of hay in the loft, and through the tiny window Heidi could see the whole valley.

Each day Peter the goatherd took his goats down to the pastures to feed, and throughout the summer Heidi went with him.

"I think Grandfather's goats, Little Bear and Little Swan, are the prettiest," Heidi said as she and Peter shared a lunch of cheese and creamy goat's milk.

Summer passed into autumn, and one day Heidi looked out
to see the top of the Alm covered with snow.

Now it was too cold for the goats to go down to the pastures,
and Peter went off to the village school instead.

Heidi, too, was busy, helping her grandfather to make cheeses, while at night they sat together around the warm stove listening to the wind in the fir trees outside.

One day Peter struggled up the snowy mountain path to ask Heidi to visit his old grandmother, who was blind.

So Heidi's grandfather got out his sledge and took Heidi down to the cottage where Peter lived with his mother and his grandmother.

Heidi loved Peter's grandmother as soon as she saw the old lady sitting at her spinning wheel.

But Heidi noticed how the cottage roof leaked and the windows rattled. So she asked her grandfather to return the next day to mend them.

"What a kind child Heidi is!" said Peter's grandmother.

Time passed happily for Heidi for she and her grandfather had come to love each other dearly.

But one day Aunt Dete returned saying that she wished to take Heidi away to Frankfurt to be the companion of the invalid daughter of a rich family.

Heidi would be taught to read and write and be treated like Clara's own sister.

The Alm Uncle refused to part with Heidi, but by a trick Aunt Dete persuaded Heidi to go with her, promising that Heidi would soon be back with fine presents for her grandfather and Peter's grandmother.

And so Heidi set off to a new life in Frankfurt.

But poor Heidi found life in a grand house very different from her carefree life on the Alm. Although she and Clara grew very fond of each other, Heidi found there were many rules to be obeyed.

Rules for getting up, going to bed . . . even for eating or keeping silent.

But Heidi also found two new friends. One was the kindly doctor who came to visit Clara regularly. He always found time to stop and speak to Heidi.

The other was Clara's grandmother, who spent many patient hours teaching Heidi to read and write.

And, of course, there was Heidi's special friend , Clara, so
pretty and sweet, but, oh, so frail, and unable to walk.

How Clara loved to hear Heidi talk about her grandfather
and life on the Alm with Peter and the goats, and dear blind
grandmother.

"Oh, how I should love to see it all!" Clara would cry.

And how Heidi echoed these thoughts silently in her heart. How she longed for her mountain home with its green valley instead of all the fine grey stone city houses. Even the golden steeple of the church gave her no joy.

Heidi grew paler and more homesick as the days passed by.

At last Clara's father grew so worried about Heidi, that he asked his old friend the doctor what he should do.

"Send her home to the Alm before she becomes really sick," urged the doctor. "Our little mountain flower is wilting badly."

So Heidi's suitcase was packed that very day so that she could return to the mountains she loved.

As Heidi kissed Clara goodbye, she promised that soon Clara should visit her.

"Our clear mountain air will make you well!" she promised.

And so it was, some time later, that as the Alm Uncle sat
smoking his pipe outside his hut, he saw something that made
him cry out with joy. Heidi was climbing up the mountain path
to the hut.

As she reached the top, she threw her arms around his neck.
"Grandfather, I have come home!" she cried.

After a while Heidi went down to see Peter and his mother and his grandmother. How happy they were to find that Heidi had returned to them.

Heidi read the grandmother beautiful hymns and she promised that she would teach Peter to read too, as a surprise for his teacher.

But happy though she was to be home, Heidi did not forget her kind friends, the Sesemanns, and she spoke about them often to her grandfather.

And one day a little procession came up the mountainside. It was Clara, in a sedan chair carried by two men, followed by a lady on a horse, a guide pushing Clara's empty wheelchair and another carrying luggage.

"Clara, you've come at last!" cried Heidi, rushing to greet her friend.

"Yes, and she is to stay for one whole month!" said Grandmamma Sesemann, as Heidi's grandfather helped her down from her horse and welcomed her warmly.

Heidi jumped about with joy at this news.

And so began a very happy time for the two friends. Each day Grandfather carried Clara down to where Peter kept his goats, and set her down on the soft grass. Clara spent the day with Peter and Heidi, making garlands for the goats to wear with the pretty flowers which Heidi picked, and breathing in the sweet mountain air.

Soon her cheeks grew rosy and her appetite grew as she drank lots of sweet goat's milk and ate thick wedges of the creamy cheese which Grandfather cut.

"Oh, Heidi, it is so lovely here," sighed Clara. "I feel so much stronger. If only I could walk down the mountain like you!"

As she looked at her friend's glowing cheeks, Heidi had an idea. She would try to help Clara to walk. So, secretly, every day, Peter and Heidi helped Clara to try to stand and walk. It was long, patient work, but at last Clara could manage to walk a short way.

When the month was ended and Mr. Sesemann came to take Clara home, what a surprise he got! Walking towards him came his own little daughter, rosy-cheeked and glowing with health.

"It is a miracle!" he gasped, clasping Clara in his arms.

"I knew the mountains would make Clara well," cried Heidi, happily. "There is no place in the world as lovely as the Alm!"